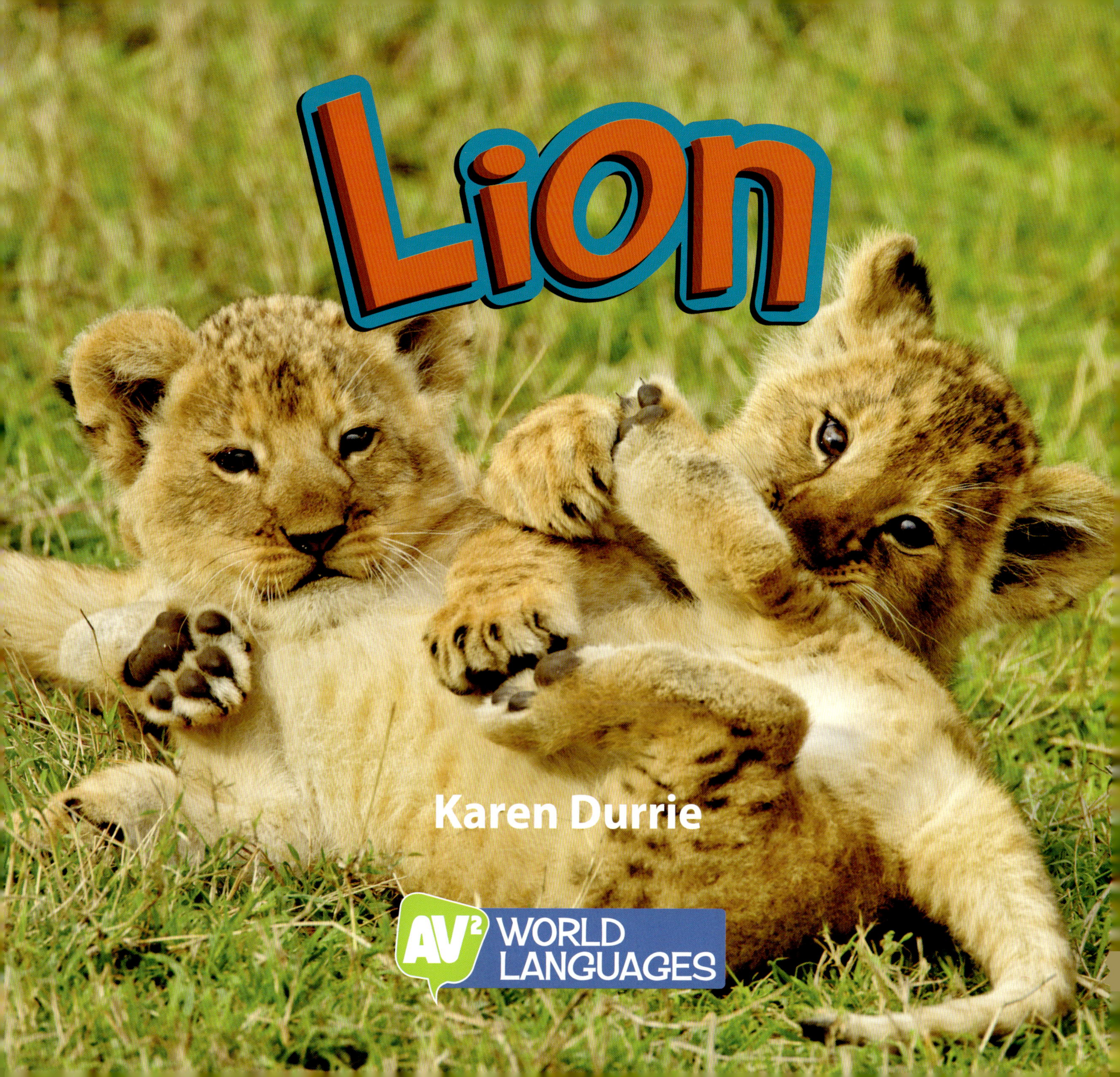
Lion
Karen Durrie
AV2 WORLD LANGUAGES

Go to **openlightbox.com**, and enter the book's unique code.

BOOK CODE

Y367225

Easily move through highly visual pages.

Toggle between your **17 books in 17 languages.**

The digital components of this book are guaranteed to stay active for at least five years from the date of publication.

This title is part of our AV2 World Languages digital subscription.

Published by AV2
276 5th Avenue, Suite 704 #917
New York, NY 10001
Website: www.openlightbox.com

Library of Congress Control Number: 2017951602

ISBN 978-1-4896-6566-9 (hardcover)
ISBN 978-1-4896-6567-6 (multi-user eBook)

Printed in Guangzhou, China
2 3 4 5 6 7 8 9 0 28 27 26 25 24

062024
240614

Project Coordinator: Karen Durrie Art Director: Terry Paulhus

Weigl acknowledges Getty Images as the primary image supplier for this title.

Access all of the AV2 World Languages titles with our digital subscription.

1-Year World Languages Subscription ISBN
978-1-4896-8345-8

Lion

In this book, I will teach you about

- myself
- my food
- my home
- my family

and much more!

I am a lion.

I am the second largest cat in the world.

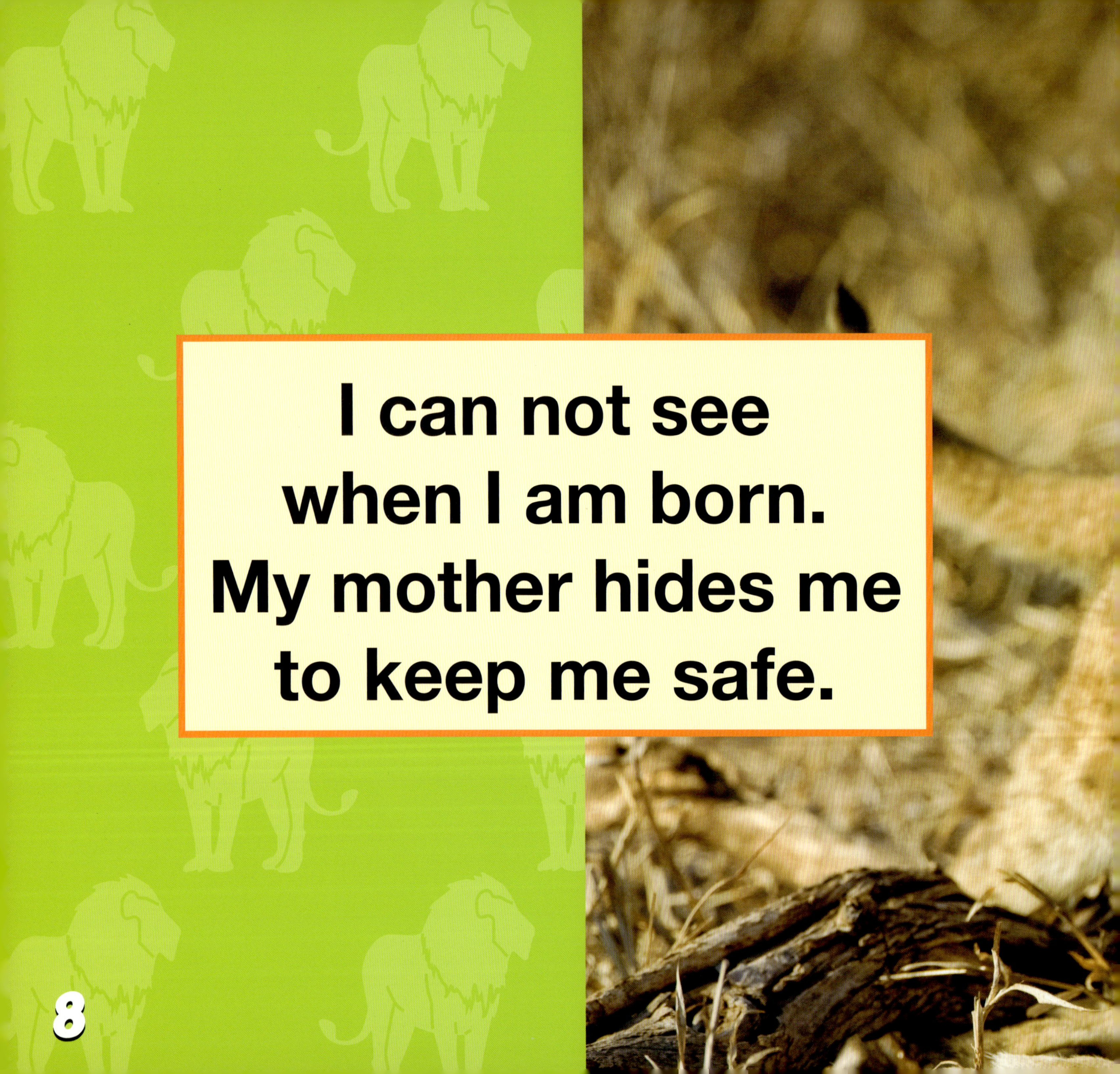

I can not see when I am born. My mother hides me to keep me safe.

I have a roar you can hear from five miles away.

I can go five days without drinking water.

I can run down
a football field
in just six seconds.

I sleep for 20 hours each day.

I can eat 75 pounds of food in one meal.

I have a long thick mane around my neck.

I am a lion.

LION FACTS

These pages provide detailed information that expands on the interesting facts found in the book. They are intended to be used by adults as a learning support to help young readers round out their knowledge of this amazing animal.

Pages 4–5

I am a lion. Lions in the wild live mostly in national parks and reserves in Africa, south of the Sahara Desert. Their habitat includes grasslands, dry woodlands, and plains. They have short, coarse fur that ranges in color from light brown to reddish gold.

Pages 6–7

Lions are the second largest cat in the world. Lions are second only to tigers in size, though lions are taller when measured shoulder to foot. The largest lion can weigh more than 600 pounds (272 kilograms) and measure 13 feet (4 meters) long from nose to tail. Female lions are smaller than males.

Pages 8–9

Lions cannot see when they are born, so the mother hides them to keep them safe. Lion cubs are born with their eyes closed. Their eyes open about 10 days after birth. Lions are born with spotted coats. The mother hides them and then introduces them to the family, called a pride, at one to two months of age.

Pages 10–11

Lions have a roar you can hear from five miles (8 kilometers) away. Lions roar to communicate with their pride, and to tell other lions where they live and how big their pride is. They also communicate by rubbing against each other, using tail signals, and making sounds such as grunts.

Pages 12–13

Lions can go five days without drinking water. Lions will drink water daily if it is nearby, but they can go four to five days without it. They can receive the moisture they need from plants and their prey.

Pages 14–15

Lions can run down a football field in just six seconds. That is a distance of 120 yards, or 110 meters. Lions can reach a speed of 50 miles (80 km) per hour. They run this fast only in short bursts, and usually only do so after sneaking up on prey.

Pages 16–17

Lions sleep for 20 hours a day. Lions are heavy and live in hot places, so they lie around and sleep to stay cool. They may only eat once every few days, so resting between meals makes the food in their stomachs last longer.

Pages 18–19

Lions can eat 75 pounds (34 kg) of food in one meal. Lions prey mostly on large mammals, including zebras, buffalo, deer, wildebeests, and warthogs. Lions often hunt in teams. It is mostly the female lions in a pride that do the hunting. They let the males eat first and the cubs last.

Pages 20–21

Lions have a long, thick mane around their neck. Lions are the only cat with a mane. Only male lions have manes. The lion population is decreasing because of hunting and loss of habitat. It is estimated there are about 39,000 wild lions left in the world. The world lion population has been cut in half since 1950.

KEY WORDS

Research has shown that as much as 65 percent of all written material published in English is made up of 300 words. These 300 words cannot be taught using pictures or learned by sounding them out. They must be recognized by sight. This book contains 38 common sight words to help young readers improve their reading fluency and comprehension. This book also teaches young readers several important content words, such as proper nouns. These words are paired with pictures to aid in learning and improve understanding.

Page	Sight Words First Appearance
4	a, am, I
6	in, second, the, world
8	can, keep, me, mother, my, not, see, to, when
10	away, from, have, hear, miles, you
12	go, days, water, without
14	down, just, run, seconds
16	each, for
18	eat, food, of, one
20	around, long

Page	Content Words First Appearance
4	lion
6	cat
8	safe
10	five, roar
14	football field, six
16	hours
18	meal, pounds
20	mane, neck